Let's Get Jumping!

Written by Melinda La Rose  Illustrated by Alan Batson

Bath • New York • Singapore • Hong Kong • Cologne • Delhi
Melbourne • Amsterdam • Johannesburg • Shenzhen

Ahoy, mateys! Do you want to join my pirate crew? Then just say the pirate password, 'yo-ho-ho!' and learn the Never Land pirate pledge.

One day, Jake and his crew are playing on the beach. Suddenly, Skully notices something. “Package, ahoy!”
“Maybe it’s treasure,” says Cubby.
“Only one way to find out,” says Jake. “Let’s open ’er up!”

"Yo-ho, way to go!" says Jake. "It's a pogo stick!"

"What are we waiting for? Let's get jumping," says Izzy.

BOING, BOING! The crew takes turns jumping.

"Coconuts!" says Cubby, losing his balance. "This pogo stick is awfully springy!"

“Don’t worry, Cubby,” says Jake. “You just need some practice.”
“I’ll try again later,” says Cubby.

"Smee, will you hold still?" says Captain Hook.

"Sorry, Cap'n, it's just that this wind is so … windy," says Smee.

"How am I ever going to get me hat down from that blasted tree?" Hook wonders aloud.

Just then, they hear … **BOING, BOING, BOING!**

"Did you see that?" asks Hook. "That puny pirate is using that *sproingy* thing to get a banana out of a tree!"

"That's nice, but I'm not ready for a snack," says Smee.

"No, you **SCURVY SEA DOG!** If I had that bouncy thing, I could get me hat!" says Hook.

Why, a pirate on a pogo stick, of course!

"WHOA!" says Cubby.

"Steady as she goes," says Jake. "You're doing great!"

YOINK! Hook uses his plunger hook to grab the pogo stick!

"Yay-hey, no way!" calls Izzy.

"That sneaky snook took our pogo stick," says Cubby.

BOING! "Look, Smee!" calls Hook. "I got me hat!"

"That's good, sir," calls Smee. "Now you'd had better stop before you hurt yourself."

"Nonsense," says Hook. "How could I possibly – ouch!"

"Smee! This blasted thing is broken," shouts Hook.
"Cap'n, where are you going?" shouts Smee.
"To get me hat!" calls Hook.

Sharky and Bones sing as the captain bounces by:

"Oh, the captain he was slick
And he nabbed a pogo stick.
A stolen stick? Why, that's a no-no.
Now he can't stop – he's bound to pogo
On his *boingy, sproingy, youchy, ouchy,* loco pogo stick!"

"Stop singing and save me, you BILGE RATS!" calls Hook.

BOING!

"Where could Captain Hook be?" Cubby wonders aloud. Just then the crew hears …

"I hear Hook, but I don't see him anywhere," says Izzy.

"Look!" says Jake. "Pogo-stick tracks. If we follow them, I bet we'll find Captain Hook!"

"And our pogo stick," says Skully.

BOING, BOING!

"AIEEEEEEE!" cries Captain Hook.
"Cap'n? Cap'n, where'd you go?" says Smee.
"Up here!" shouts Hook.

"I'll throw down the *sproingy, boingy* thing and you jump up here and get me," says Hook.

 Smee bounces up, but he can't reach!

"Smee," shouts Captain Hook, "can't you do anything right?"

"There's Mr Smee," says Izzy.

"And our pogo stick!" says Skully.

"Thank goodness you sea pups are here," says Smee. "Here's your pogo stick. Sorry for all the trouble."

"That's okay, Mr Smee," says Jake. "Thanks for returning our pogo stick."

"Um, there's just one little problem," says Smee. "I'm afraid the Cap'n is, well … up a tree."

"CRACKERS!" says Skully. "A pirate in a tree? Now I've seen everything!"

How did Hook feel when they took the pogo stick?

"Can you help him get down?" asks Smee.

"I don't need their help!" cries Hook. "I can get down on my … WHOOOOOAAAAAAAAA!"

"Oh, no," says Cubby. "He's going to fall!"

"We have to help him – and fast," says Jake.

“I know what will help Captain Hook get out of that tree,” says Izzy. “Pixie dust!”

“Come on, Mr Smee,” says Jake.

Izzy sprinkles everyone with pixie dust!

“Oh, my, I can fly!” says Smee.

"I don't need help," says Hook. "I'm fi – *ahhh!*"
Izzy sprinkles Hook with pixie dust just in time!
"Did I crash?" asks Hook.
"No, sir," says Smee. "Look!"

"I'M FLYING!" says Hook.

"Time to fly back to Pirate Island!" says Jake.

"Thanks for your help, sea pups," says Smee. "Now let's find your hat, Cap'n."

What did the ocean say to the flying pirate?

"What do you say, Cubby? Ready to give that pogo stick another try?" asks Izzy.

"I guess," says Cubby. He gets on and takes a few hops.

BOING, BOING, BOING!

"Woo-hoo! Look at me! I'm a pogo master!" calls Cubby.

"I knew you'd get the hang of it if you tried," says Jake.

Nothing.
It just waved.

“Now that I have my hat back, I’m as handsome as ever,” says Captain Hook.

“Oh, yes, Cap’n, you’re a looker, you are,” says Smee.

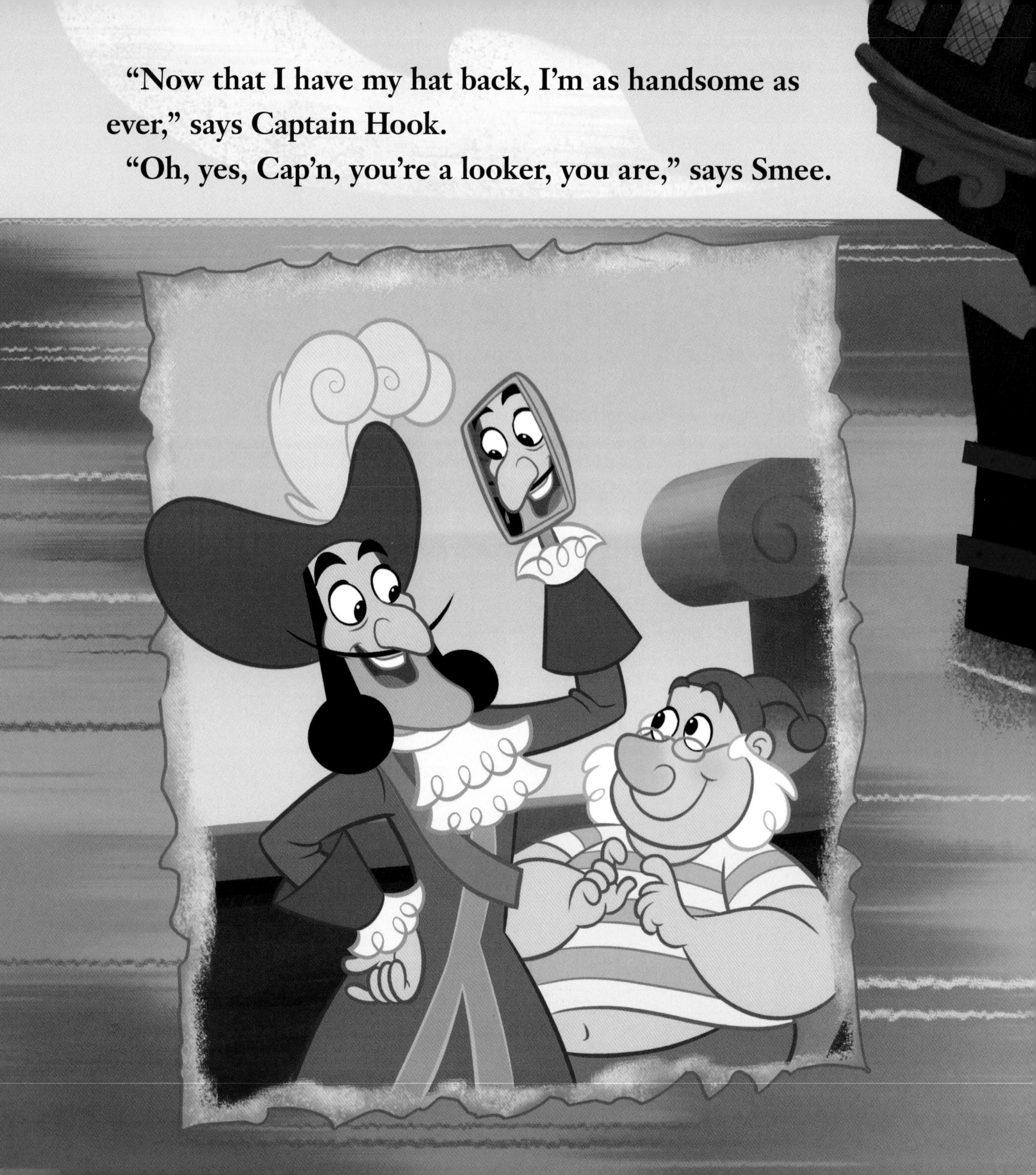

WOOOOOOSSSSSSHHHHHHHH!

A gust of wind blows Hook's hat right off his head!

"BARNACLES! Not again," says Hook. "Catch that hat!"

"Aye, aye, Cap'n," says Smee. "Oh, look, sir, here it is, right on top of the water."

Smee is about to grab the hat when he hears …

"Mr Crocodile," says Smee, "may I have that hat back … please?"

SNAP! The croc snaps his teeth.

"On second thought, you know, that hat looks really good on you," says Smee. "Don't you think so, Cap'n?"

"Oh, yes, very fashionable," says Hook. "N-n-now be a g-g-good crocodile and swim away!"

Back on Pirate Island . . .

"You know," says Jake, "if Hook had just asked for help in the first place, he wouldn't have gotten into all that trouble."

"And we wouldn't have lost our pogo stick," says Skully.

“Check it out!” says Jake. “For solving pirate problems today, we earned some Gold Doubloons!”

“Let’s open the Team Treasure Chest and count ’em,” says Cubby.

"Way to go, mateys!" says Jake. "We earned eight Gold Doubloons!"

"I did it!" calls Cubby. "Whee!"